Jaded

By Earvin Phillip Eugene

Commencement

Jordan Williams attended Dartmouth college. He worked at Zimmerman Fitness Center. Jordan needed the money and it was his opportunity to meet colleagues. He was about 5'11, brown-skinned with short black curly hair. Jordan sported glasses as he was near-sighted and groomed himself with a goatee. He wore outlandish fashion with striking designs such as a red and black flannel sweatshirt alongside checkered pants. On some days he would dress in Dartmouth green apparel, but today was a special day. Jordan had to spend time with his girlfriend, Mae, it was there one-year anniversary.

Jordan was walking through campus passing by the "Dartmouth Green" on his way to School House where he resides. His room was simple with a desk and bed. He had vintage posters of the Beatles and Muhammad Ali. He was a "classic man". Atop of his bed was a Ghana flag as his parents were immigrants and he was first generation African American. He was proud of his ancestry; being 41% Ghana, 25% Cameroon-Congo, 10% British (Anglo-Saxon), 10% Benin-Togo, 3%

French, 2% Nigerian, 2% Greece-Albanian, 2% Portuguese, 2% Senegal, 2% Irish Celtic, and 1% Slavic as reported by AncestryDNA. As many other black people, he was unaware of his diverse cultural background but was curious to trace his roots.

The quad was placed with four roommates including Jordan, Alex, I.T., and Asim. Alex Fischer was a first generation American with his parents from Romania. He grew up in Newtown, Connecticut. Alex was smaller in stature, with a height of 5'6. He had dark brown hair and bright green eyes. Alexander exercised frequently and followed a specific diet regimen. He only ate fruits and vegetables during the week. He majored in business and was more of a serious fellow. Jordan told Alex "let's drink a few beers and watch The Killing of a Sacred Deer on Netflix". Alex agreed and said, "why not". It was Friday and it was routine for them to relax from a rough week. Jordan believed this gave him enough time to unwind before Mae would arrive in the evening. Alex used to be a party animal in the beginning of college, but now became more studious and reserved. Jordan believed ritually in drinking to share fun moments.

Jordan studied biology with a minor in writing. He was a renaissance man. His goal is to become a scientific writer for the Food & Drug Administration. His family advising him to go into medicine like his uncles. Jordan stated "Martin" from The Killing of a Sacred Deer was "creepy, something is off about him." Alex found entertainment in "Steven Murphy" sex scene with his wife "Anna". Alex proclaimed, "Nicole Kidman is hot!" They both laughed and agreed. Alex continued to simultaneously work on school assignments and surf the internet on his laptop as he watched the movie. Jordan decided to have a few more Keystone beers. He became noticeably drunk. Alex did not mind; he enjoyed the company instead of his usual solitude.

Mae arrived at the door. Jordan is quite functional drunk; except he becomes slightly sloppy with his actions and motives. He rejoiced to open the door and see Mae. He declared his affection for her by giving a strong hug and saying, "How are you baby?" She showed disapproval of his state by accepting the hug, but not returning it. She stated, "What are we going to do for our anniversary?" Mae has always been straightforward, Jordan liked that about her. He was amused by her frustration against her petite physique. Jordan smiled and said, "We could go to a frat party at Alpha Chi Alpha." She agreed. Mae went to the refrigerator and began to drink a Keystone beer. They were past the nights of strong liquor at dorm parties from their freshman years and started to broaden their horizons at frat parties. There were things to do and people to meet on campus nowadays. Mae walked to Jordan's bedroom away from the common area to talk as Jordan prepared for their night out. She used to play soccer in high school, which explained her slim and athletic appearance. It also provided her confidence from being a team leader. Her childhood consisted of traveling across the country in tournaments with teammates and her parents. Mae was very knowledgeable but not the ambitious type academically in her youth. It was a way of revolting from her father, a reputable biology professor at Stony Brook University. Her resume was salvaged with plenty of extracurricular activities. Including the fact, she had guidance from her dad to attend Stony Brook University. See, Mae's education was at Stony Brook Preparatory High School and Jordan at Ward Melville High School. Two neighboring schools on Long Island, New York. In fact, that is how they met at a joint high school party one Summer senior year. They dated but had a long-distance relationship for some time. Mae at Stony Brook University for Freshman and Sophomore year before transferring to Dartmouth. And Jordan spending his complete time there. It was a matter of time before their combined efforts would place them together. It was not enough to see each other during the offseason of college. Mae mentioned a good poem from Rupi Kaur of "Milk and Honey" and described new hip-hop songs she heard from "The Weeknd". Jordan interestingly listened, while looking at her light brown eyes with freckles. She played with her dark brown hair as he finished getting ready.

Asim entered the dorm. He was of average height and build. His family was of Indian descent. He was personable and a fair-minded person. Asim was Muslim in faith and therefore did not drink alcohol.

This was different from most of the Dartmouth student body. However, he did vape and preferred hookah when given the opportunity. Alex said, "What's up bud?" Asim stated, "Bro I just got a blitzy (Blitzmail) from lips (Amy)". They called her lips simply for the characteristic of her full lips. She was a mixed beauty of Asian and Hispanic heritage. All the guys in School House wanted to spend time with her. Alex was not surprised and said, "She wants you dude, what did she say?" Asim spoke aloud, "These are the lips, powerful rudders pushing through groves of kelp, this girl's terrible, unsweetened taste of the whole ocean, its fathoms: **this is that taste**." Jordan entered the common area and proclaimed, "Lips is aware of her lips" and laughed. Mae stated "you guys are stupid, Asim I think you two are a good match. I can put in a good word for you." As she reached in the fridge for one more Keystone. Asim started inhaling from his Juul and mentioned his satisfaction. Alex would play "Reckless" by Arin Ray on YouTube on the Smart TV to set the pregame mood as he finished his beer. He rejoiced "Asim's got it made". Jordan began to take a few puffs from Asim's vape and stated, "Alex good choice". They would all continue with banter alongside different fun and melodic music. Vaping and drinking beers until about 9:30 at night when Jordan stated, "We better head out." In a calm and friendly manner, Jordan and Mae left the dorm. Alex and Asim went to their separate rooms.

Party Favor

It was Springtime in Hanover, New Hampshire. The weather was cool on this night. Much warmer than the difficult Winters. Jordan and Mae enjoyed the fresh air of New England. The Alpha Chi Alpha party was full of vibrant faces and excited individuals. The house had a pungent smell of stale beer. Music was loud and energetic. It was Dartmouth tradition to play beer pong without the handle of the paddle. It was a fun twist to the game. Jordan being a Senior had the experience to play along with other Seniors. Mae was his partner on the table, and they were a great duo.

Later in the night, full of drunken spirit the two wanted to sober up and find time alone. They made it just in time to the Pine for a quick meal. They had the Grab N' Go that included cheeseburger and fries.

They usually preferred the Courtyard Café, but tonight was a special occasion. On the way back to School House, Jordan gave Mae a Pandora charm bracelet. She embraced him with a kiss. In the moment she was full of bliss. Girls like things. This gift would buy her affection for at least a week. Mae was thankful, but accustomed to receiving gifts.

They arrived back at School House and ate their food enjoying the quietness. It was a sincere moment between two lovers. After the meal, Jordan asked Mae, "Do you love me?" She answered, "I do." They went to the bedroom and began to undress. Mae was beautiful naked with subtle freckles and tan skin. Jordan with his strong shape, grabbed her and they made love.

Once they finished, Mae rested her head onto Jordan's chest for quite some time. Mae got dressed as they both had few inhalations of Jordan's vape. She left into the night. Once alone with his thoughts, Jordan went through his stash and found his half-finished bottle of Chairman's Reserve Rum. He received it during a past family trip to St.

Lucia. He took a few swigs to end the night. After all, today was a day of celebration.

In the morning, Jordan followed his typical routine of vaping and drinking tea. He was met by his roommate I.T., he must have arrived at some point last night. I.T. was a Nigerian whose name stood for Ifedolapo Tijani. He was six feet tall right on the nose. Tall and dark-skinned with unmatched white bright teeth. He was plainly muscular with little effort to exercise or conditioning. He possessed an accent and was the most mature of the group. I.T. stated, "You have fun last night?" Jordan in a joking manner, "It was the time of my life." Tijani shared political commentary on politics and Trump. He mostly described satire of the president suggesting administering disinfectants like Lysol and Clorox to treat Coronavirus infections. Jordan was amused and mentioned how Trump is the funniest president ever.

The discussion became more serious when Jordan explained he needed to get something off his chest. He began to describe the night a few weeks ago when he attended a party at Kappa Kappa Kappa with his friend Jared. They competed for this pretty and captivating girl. Jordan made a pass at her, commenting on the fact that "She was not one for emptying her face of expression." Her face was evenly symmetric and resembled a lively Logan Laurice Browning. She brought him to a private room for what Jordan thought would be a romantic linkage. However, she described to him of his wrongdoing in praising women solely on their physical appearance. He was distraught and responded by saying "I want to get to know you." The girl stated, "I am not the type of girl for you" and kissed him on the cheek. This left Jordan more fascinated by her. Jared would have several failed attempts at the girl before they both surrendered.

Jordan felt guilty in his aspirations of girls while still being in a long-lasting relationship. I.T. reassured him of all men's shortcomings in this matter. He said "You're young, but you love her" regarding Mae. Jordan simply agreed. In order to ease tension, he illustrated how the frat party host placed dirty socks in the alcohol punch bowl before the gathering and advised him with caution to drink on that night. It is safe to say, Jordan only drank from Keystone beer cans. Ifedolapo laughed and said, "only at Dartmouth".

Hiatus

It was Spring Break and Jordan was back on Long Island. He spent time with his childhood friend Joseph. They would go to his basement and smoke "Blue Dream" from the bong. This became their recreation ever since they both graduated high school. They played FIFA on the Xbox. Jordan was better at the game than Joseph, but it was just a means to pass time. Joseph prided himself on being a good host. He mixed some Long Island Iced Teas and shared stories from the past. Whether it be, Joseph's past prowess as a football player or the times they both attended their school's county lacrosse games yearly at Stony Brook University. It was good to be back home.

Joseph's older brother, Matthew, was visiting from New Jersey and arrived in the basement for greetings. He hovered over the two. Tall in stature. He was a funny and athletic fellow. Matthew announced, "What's up pussies?" and took part in the festivities. In customary fashion, he bragged of his past achievements. Whether it be about the women he managed to conquer or the championships from lax. He beat Jordan in FIFA and reminded him of his years of experience with the game. Matthew represented the relic of the "Long Island Bro". He mentioned to them his bachelor's party arrangement because he was to be married to his longtime girlfriend and fiancé. The two brothers discussed the savage time they would have in Atlantic City to celebrate. There would be girls, gambling, and cocaine. Jordan had to go back to school for graduation, so he could not make it. In addition, he never did anything pass weed. Joseph being more experienced proposed Jordan try magic mushrooms, "it's a life changing opportunity." They decided for Joe to buy the stuff so Jordan could give it a try.

Certain plans changed when Jordan wished to try shrooms with Mae. They determined it was best to do it in an open serene place. Mae suggested Avalon Park in old historic Stony Brook. Mae was skeptical in trying psychedelic drugs, just like Jordan she only experimented with marijuana. She recalled the time Jordan and she had brownies and thought it would be similar. They laughed and cried tears of joy. Mae was open-minded and she could not think of a better thing to do with her boyfriend on Spring Break.

It was a bright sunny day and all the flowers were blooming at Avalon. The scenery was very versatile. It started at a bridge that mimicked a Japanese garden. There was a beautiful arrangement of sparkling colors. The water underneath the bridge had synchronous waves with the wind as if the earth itself was breathing. Next, followed the stone steps. Hard and very symmetric. Above reached a replica ritual circle from some ancient civilization. It was composed of stone and grass. In the past the two took for granted the spiritual representation of the site. After, they reached what appeared to imitate farmland. Yellow wheatgrass flowed around the dirt path. They truly felt isolated as it seemed few people were on the path today. There was a sense of excitement and pleasure mixed against melancholy. Stumbling through the majestic path, they arrived at tranquil shrubbery. The environment was lush green and at the center a blue pond. Colors like on a canvas were noticeable throughout the surrounding. In the moment there was bliss. Jordan and Mae absorbed the animals and nature. They decided to go back to the entrance. Time felt as it was rewinding as the two held hands for reassurance walking back. By the gateway it seemed as if the roads were slowly oscillating. The pavement appeared to have dramatic humps. In a state of panic Jordan and Mae rushed into his car. Sitting in the backseat, a British police officer strolled past as something seen from a stereotypical image on Google. He wore a bobby on the beat and held an old school Billy Club. They were shocked. A few steps behind the officer was a brown man of Sikh faith. They were in awe of what they were seeing. It could not be possible. In order to calm down they stared at their iPhones. The devices possessed magical pixel colors. Mae suggested they get fresh air outside the car when the coast seemed clear. They felt calmer. Jordan and Mae viewed each other. Mae said, "You look stunning." She described how he looked so young and high-spirited. His skin was shiny and clear of blemishes. As Jordan looked at Mae, he stated, "You look remarkable!" Apparently, each brown strand of hair was noticeable. He could imagine her as an old woman and she still seemed beautiful. Still high, they discussed driving back to Jordan's home to end this escapade. Mae was determined to drive Jordan's car nervously. She forcibly stated, "Jordan the reality of the situation is you are black, and I don't want you to get arrested for driving under the influence." Jordan was upset but did not feel this was the time and place to have an enduring argument of the complexities of racial injustice in America, so he receded. Mae drove, as they were still tripping. They arrived safe and sound at Jordan's house. They were relieved. His parents were watching television. Mae and Jordan, he heated up a frozen pizza and went to Jordan's room. He was impressed by her courage. The exchanged remarks about the whole experience. They ate the pizza, which seemed more delicious than usual. Jordan kissed Mae, and they made love with the remnants of the high. The sex was more caring compared to other times.

Convocation

It was time for graduation. Everyone on campus was covered in green and black caps and gowns. Alex and Jordan sneaked cigarettes by the campus in the morning. Sometimes there is no substitute for the real thing. Jordan sprayed himself with Polo Red by Ralph Lauren cologne to hide his misbehavior. He shared a few shots of his rum with I.T. and Alex, as Asim drank Red bull and vaped at the dorm.

They each discussed what they would do after graduation. Alex would apply to be a consultant with his economics degree at Bain Capital in Boston, Massachusetts. He mentioned an alumnus of the firm, "Mitt Romney made it there, so can I". Asim, who studied Political Science and Government, would become a public policy analyst before tossing his hat in the ring at law school, preferably, Columbia University. Ifedolapo as a computer science engineer had his sights set at Google. Finally, Jordan with mixed feelings from his passion and family pressure believed he would take a year off to travel and drink. Realistically, he knew that he would work with his family's support until he was ready to apply to medical school. This depressed him. He made a cheer to the future with his friends.

The ceremony was splendid. All his close ones were present. His father, mother, older brother, and younger sister were all there to witness his success. Mae and her family were in attendance as well. Mae with her psychology background would work under her father and perhaps take a children's psychologist job in the meantime before applying to medical school to become a psychiatrist. Her father wanted his daughter to have the interactive skills of a professor, while the lucrative position of a doctor.

The guest speaker spoke of perseverance and ambition in life. The possibilities for the future being endless. A quote from Dr. Seuss stroke attention, "You're off to Great Places! Today is your day! Your mountain is waiting, So... get on your way!" The calling of names for diplomas would ensue. Jordan, Mae, and all their friends received mentions. Everyone was ecstatic and grateful. One of Jordan's favorite professors stated, "Don't cry because it's over. Smile because it happened" and handed him a fine cigar. The moment was profound.

Upon returning to Long Island for the Summer, Jordan met with his cousin to drink and smoke cigars at the harbor to celebrate. He too just graduated UCLA with a bachelor's in history. They roamed around the area puffing their tobacco. James, his cousin, discussed the last great American president was Kennedy. To evade the Cuban Missile Crisis, help the disenfranchised during the Civil Rights era, and the fact that he intellectualized international and domestic affairs at the ripe age of forty-three years old.

The two entered the Brewology bar at Port Jefferson, this time Jordan shared scientific facts about ethanol metabolism. He described how alcohol is degraded by an enzyme called alcohol dehydrogenase. The alcohol is changed to acetaldehyde, next to acetate, and finally into carbon dioxide and water. He paraphrased that ethanol is the intoxicating part of alcohol and as it reaches the brain, it interferes with normal neurotransmission. Jordan said, "Here's to alcohol, the rose-colored glasses of life" with a smile. That day was especially good, so he thought.

Jordan ended the evening by spending time with Mae at West Meadow Beach. Usually, the place was delightful, many great memories were shared there, however in this occasion it felt somber. She had bad news. Mae told Jordan she was pregnant. Jordan stayed calm and said, "We'll take care of it". Mae cried, but knew it was best. She was upset but realized she was not alone in the matter. This would be the most difficult part of their relationship with constant bickering and slight comments. Deep down they knew the real issue was the unborn child, but it was not something they had the maturity to debate. The two resolved the problem in the coming week, so they thought. After the ordeal, the partnership was never the same. Whether it be due to the nerve-wrecking and painful process of an abortion or because they felt what was the point of a relationship that did not lead to family and marriage. Within a few months, the relationship met its end.

Without the support of a loving companion and the pressures of the world after graduation Jordan confided in the bottle. He drank strong liquor at home. Sometimes friends would stop by to hangout and family encouraged him to be productive, but nobody knew his pain. One night

fueled by sleep deprivation, sadness, and drunkenness he started a

heated argument with his family. His parents and siblings were scared

for Jordan's health with nothing left to do they provided police and

ambulance support to take him to the hospital.

Not Oneself

Psychiatric emergency at the hospital was a place unknown to

Jordan. As he sobered up, he was alarmed and worried. The staff

provided him Ativan to calm his nerves. Jordan had to strip down to his

underwear and was observed for physical harm or any potential

weapons. He dressed himself in scrubs and had to spend several nights

with other patients. Some were criminals and others were deranged.

Healthcare professionals viewed them from a safe and protective barrier,

only contacting them to administer medications or perform quick psych

evaluations. During his stint at the emergency hospital he got involved

in an altercation with another patient. A guy tried to push Jordan around

because he stood out like a sore thumb, several patients for some reason or another disliked him. They de-escalated the situation and injected Jordan with drugs. In a drowsy state, he walked to his hospital bed and knowing he would soon be unconscious. He was left in a haze of security, doctors, and nurses attending to him.

Jordan was transported to a behavioral psych and rehabilitation center. It was different than anything he was accustomed to but there was a strict regimen. The daily routine consisted of smoking in the gated courtyard, breakfast with medications, recreation, lunch, entertainment and counseling, dinner with medications and another smoke break. It was a glance into the real world. Patients were homeless taking advantage of the system they were given, entitled people with a dysfunctional background like Jordan, and in general individuals down on their luck. One thing they all had in common was they all were suffering in one form or another. On his first night, a bum offered him alcohol in which he managed to sneak into the premises. If Jordan were not about his wits and truly attempting to make a change in his life, he would have indulged.

In the morning, a cigarette to adjust to his new setting. Surprisingly, a healthy breakfast with eggs, milk, and fruit. Drugs that altered his mind and thoughts, presumably for the better. A short time of television in the common area, in which the seniors controlled the channels. There was a hierarchy of the patients at the hospital. Those who not only suffered from mental illness but performed some criminal acts on the outside or were simply strong in figure to demand authority. The true power lied with the healthcare professionals who could command rule with the force of security disguised as aides. If you fell from favor of the doctors or nurses, one could be subjected to an injection for bad behavior. Jordan did his best to stay calm and focused. For recreation, he kept a journal to track his thoughts, daily occurrences, and possible improvements in his actions. For lunch, he planned with the dietician to have salads. One of the patients who was ignorant to the guidelines to adjust his diet with the nutritionist was upset to see Jordan eating a salad and he spit on him from across the cafeteria. The aides detained him as the nurses injected him with a mixture of Depakote and Ativan for his misbehavior and he was left to rest in his room. Before counseling, he talked on the phone with his parents. They ensured him to stay strong and to continue with the treatment.

At counseling, the psychiatrist and social worker described to him that he suffers from depression and schizophrenia. They came to this conclusion since Jordan did not keep the best hygiene during his stay. His facial hair was unmanaged, displaying an unkept beard. His nails were not as clean as usual. He presented with delusions that people at the hospital disliked him. Jordan said, "I'm piece of shit." The doctor privately consoled to him that he reminded him of his son and reassured him that things will get better in time.

After dinner, one of the patients, who was short but strong physically played chess with him. Jordan soundly won at the game and the patient became furious. The patient forced him into the hallway and punched him in the gut. The patient was attacked and detained. He was medicated and stripped himself naked on his hospital bed before he was tied down. He was unconscious with an erection on the bed. Obviously, the patient was ill and possessed a sick sense of humor. Much of the staff were amused and laughed. The men were glad that he was obstructed, and the women were appalled. Jordan relaxed for a short period of time in the recreational area and reflected. Jordan smoked his cigarette, took his medications, and slept the night away.

Most days at the center were the same. Jordan's parents visited more often over time to check on his development. He prepared to leave, and one kind patient gave him the shirt on his back for good fortune. One nurse gave remarks of how much she is going to miss Jordan. All he could think of how far he came. He was hopeful for the future, but he was jaded.